T.G. and MOONIE
Have a Baby

Story by Fay Maschler

Pictures by
SYLVIE SELIG

Doubleday & Company, Inc.

Garden City, New York

Also by Fay Maschler and Sylvie Selig

T.G. AND MOONIE MOVE OUT OF TOWN
T.G. AND MOONIE GO SHOPPING

ISBN: 0-385-15332-5 Trade
       0-385-15333-3 Prebound
Library of Congress Catalog Card Number 79-3951
Text Copyright © 1979 by Fay Maschler
Illustrations Copyright © 1979 by Sylvie Selig

First Edition in the United States of America
Printed in Great Britain

The postman brings a letter
addressed to T.G. and Moonie.
It is from Moonie's cousin, Fraser,
saying, "Expect to see me Wednesday."
Wednesday is in two days' time.

T.G. and Moonie make the
guest room ready: clean sheets
on the bed, fresh curtains
at the window and flowers
in the vase. Bernard,
the owl who lives with
T.G. and Moonie,
wants to hang some
pictures of his family.
"Fraser will be
interested to hear about
my relatives if, as you
say, he is a cat of the
world."

T.G. decides to build a
garden seat so that they
can enjoy the fresh air.
He's read how to do it in
a do-it-yourself book.
I could do it better myself,
thinks Blott, their pet, as
he looks for the nails that
are sinking into the snow.
Moonie takes a little nap
while the sun is still warm.

On Wednesday morning
Fraser arrives by taxi just
as Bernard is getting back
from his nighttime rounds
on the blue two-wheeler bike.
Fraser has four pieces of
luggage. "I wonder how long
he plans to stay," says
Blott to no one in
particular.

Moonie is thrilled to see
her cousin, who has been away
traveling for years.
"This is T.G., my husband,"
she says, as T.G. comes
clattering down the stairs.
"Glad to meet you, T.G.,"
says Fraser. "And I am Blott,"
mutters Blott. Bernard starts
to bring in the luggage.
The house is filling up.

After supper Fraser gets out
his guitar. Country and Western
music is his strong point.
Bernard surprises everyone
by being very accomplished
on the clarinet. "Do you know
Owl Lang Syne?" he asks.
"Ssshh," says T.G. "Moonie
has nodded off to sleep.
She's very dozy lately.
I hope she's all right."
"Know what I think,
T.G.?" says Fraser.
"I think my cousin,
your wife, is going
to have a baby."

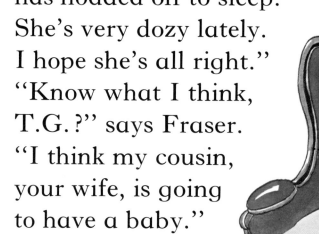

T.G. has turned the wooden
garden seat into a crib.
Thinking it's a wheelbarrow,
Moonie fills it with leaves.
Meanwhile Fraser catches up
on the foreign news in
the paper. There are
record temperatures
in Peru.

Fraser decides he will weave a
baby basket, using skills he
picked up when he was living
with South American Indians.
In and out, in and out. I see
how you do it, thinks Blott.
"At last someone has had the sense
to get a wastepaper basket,"
sighs Moonie later, and she
sorts through last week's
papers.

T.G. gets out his mail-order catalog and sends away for the very best baby basket. He explains to Moonie what they suspect. "A baby," says Moonie. "Well, that's a relief. I thought I was getting lazy or something. Oh, T.G., imagine us having a baby."

Meanwhile, the basket from the
mail-order catalog has arrived.
This is an O.K. bed they've
got for me, thinks Blott, and
he moves in his precious
blanket. Fraser starts to knit
(something he learned during
a winter in the
Hebrides), and
bootees, shawls
and mittens begin
to pile up.
"That's right,
Moonie,
take it easy,"
whispers T.G.

The next evening Moonie leaves
the table in the middle of
supper and goes upstairs.
T.G. tries to stay calm
as he busies himself washing
the dishes, but a saucer
slips from his nervous and
soapy fingers. "Nothing to
worry about," shouts Fraser,
"babies are born every day."
I wonder how I can help,
thinks Bernard, as he dries
a plate.

Moonie calls T.G.
and he races upstairs.
"Do you like the name Katherine?"
she asks. "Yes," says T.G.,
gazing at her.
"And I like Katherine too.
But where's she going
to sleep?"

Bernard arrives carrying a beautiful big bird's nest lined with downy feathers, as soft as a spring day. Katherine will fit in perfectly. "She can borrow my blanket for a bit," says Blott, "though I'll miss it at night." T.G. can't take his eyes off Katherine.

Bernard and Fraser play her a
lullaby on clarinet and guitar.
T.G. doesn't know the words
but he hums along with the tune.
Oh dear, that's making me
feel sleepy again,
thinks Moonie. But she
has every right to be.

The next evening Fraser is packed
and ready to go. "Must you?"
says Moonie. "I'll be writing,"
says Fraser, "but there's a
yacht race in Mexico that I
wouldn't miss for anything.
Take care of Katherine and
tell her who made the
bootees and the mittens,
the leggings and the jumper."
"I'll give you a hand to
the door," says T.G.

The taxi with the same driver
is waiting. Bernard leaves
for his nighttime rounds.

A family to come home
to, he thinks.
What could be better?